Anonymus

Pen drawings,

being the originals of the photo-relief cuts in part II, Vol. I Medical history

Anonymus

Pen drawings,
being the originals of the photo-relief cuts in part II, Vol. I Medical history

ISBN/EAN: 9783742821232

Manufactured in Europe, USA, Canada, Australia, Japa

Cover: Foto ©Andreas Hilbeck / pixelio.de

Manufactured and distributed by brebook publishing software
(www.brebook.com)

Anonymus

Pen drawings,

Pen Drawings,

⟞being the⟝

ORIGINALS of the PHOTO-RELIEF CUTS.

⟞in⟝

PART II. Vol. I. MEDICAL HISTORY.

See p. XII of that Work.

Diagram showing the monthly ratio of the cases of diarrhœa and dysentery among colored troops.

——— ATLANTIC REGION.　　　　　　----------- CENTRAL REGION.

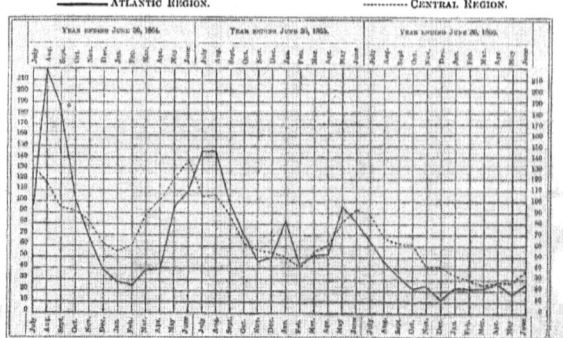

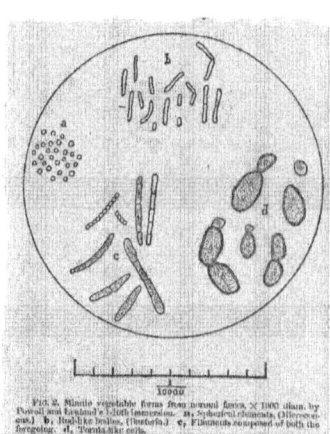

Fig. 2. Minute vegetable forms from bowel fæces, $\times$ 1000 diam. by Powell and Lealand's 1-16th immersion. *a*, Spherical elements, (Micrococcus.) *b*, Rod-like bodies, (Bacteria.) *c*, Filaments composed of both the foregoing. *d*, Torula-like cells.

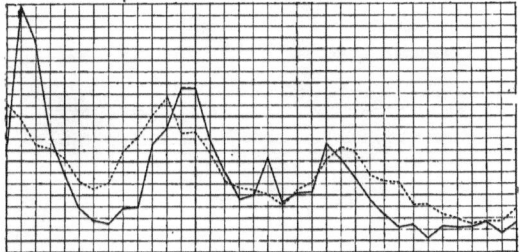

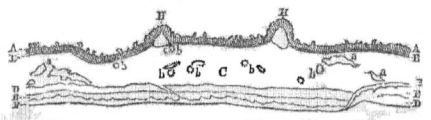

Fig. 3. Diagram explanatory of the plate facing page 328. A. Mucous membrane, with glands of Lieberkühn and villi. B. Muscle of Brücke. C. Submucous connective tissue, showing at *a, a, a,* accidental rests, and at *b, b, b, b,* bloodvessels, cut across. D. Circular muscular coat. E. Longitudinal muscular coat. F. Subperitoneal connective tissue.

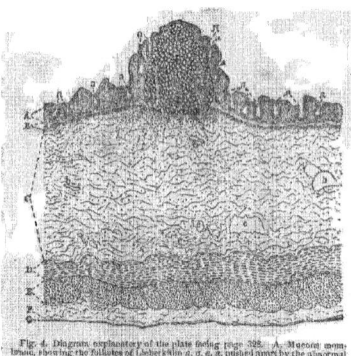

Fig. 4. Diagram explanatory of the plate facing page 328. A. Mucous membrane, showing the follicles of Lieberkühn *a, a, a,* pushed apart by the abnormal growth of adenoid tissue. B. Muscle of Brücke. C. Submucous connective tissue, showing sections of bloodvessels, as at *b, b,* and some accidental rests; as at *c, c, c.* D. Circular layer of the muscular coat of the intestine. E. Longitudinal layer. F. Subperitoneal connective tissue. G. Peritoneum. H. Enlarged solitary gland. The cells of the epithelium, adenoid tissue and solitary gland in this diagram are much exaggerated in size, and, of course, correspondingly few in number.

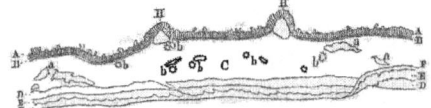

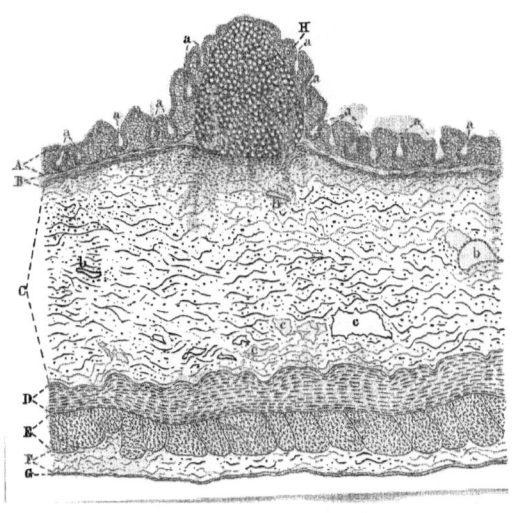

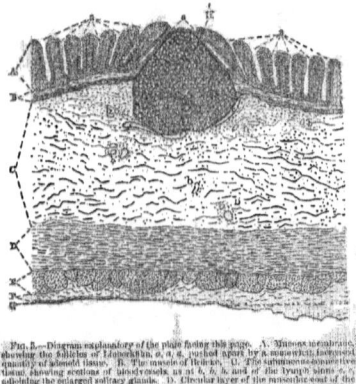

FIG. 5.—Diagram explanatory of the plate facing this page. A. Mucous membrane, showing the follicles of Lieberkühn, o, o, o, pushed apart by a somewhat increased quantity of adenoid tissue. B. The muscle of Brücke. C. The submucous connective tissue, showing sections of blood-vessels, as at b, b, b, and of the lymph sinus c, c, adjoining the enlarged solitary glands. D. Circular layer of the muscular coat of the intestine. E. Longitudinal layer. F. Subperitoneal connective tissue. G. Peritoneum. H. Enlarged solitary follicle. The cells of the epithelium, adenoid tissue, and solitary gland in this diagram are much exaggerated in size and, of course correspondingly few in number.

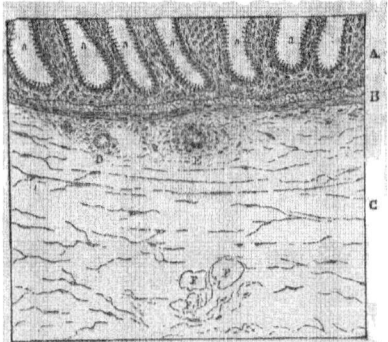

FIG. 6.—Diagram explanatory of the plate facing this page. A. Mucous membrane; a, a, a, a, follicles of Lieberkühn pushed apart by the access of new elements in the adenoid tissue. B. Muscle of Brücke. C. Submucous connective tissue. D. A small artery. E. A small vein surrounded by the lymph-cell sheath. F, F. Accidental rents in the sections. This diagram is drawn from the preparation represented in the upper figure of the plate facing this page, but will serve also to interpret the lower figure, and also the two figures in the plate facing page 331.

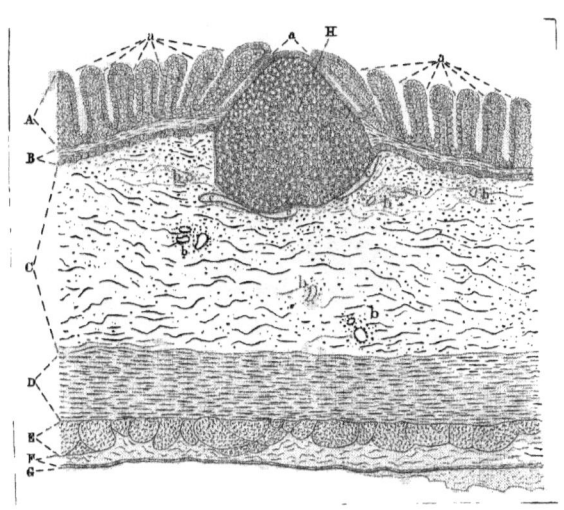

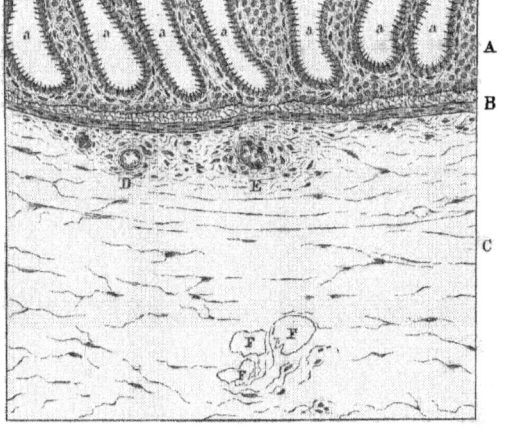

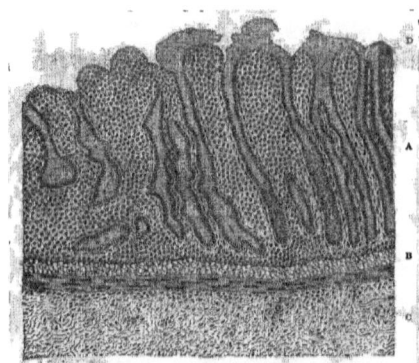

FIG. 7.—Perpendicular section of a dysenteric colon, cut longitudinally. Magnified 110 diameters. The figure is reproduced from a photo-micrograph (Neg. 913, N. S.) of No. 717. Microscopical Section.   A. Mucous membrane, showing the glands of Lieberkühn pushed abnormally apart by an accumulation of lymphoid elements in the adenoid layer. On the left and in the middle of the portion shown, several of the follicles have undergone more or less cystic distension. B. The two layers of the muscle of Brücke. C. Submucous connective tissue with an accumulation of new elements, just below the muscle of Brücke. D, Diphtheritic layer (portions of which have been lost) continuous with the contents of some of the glands of Lieberkühn.

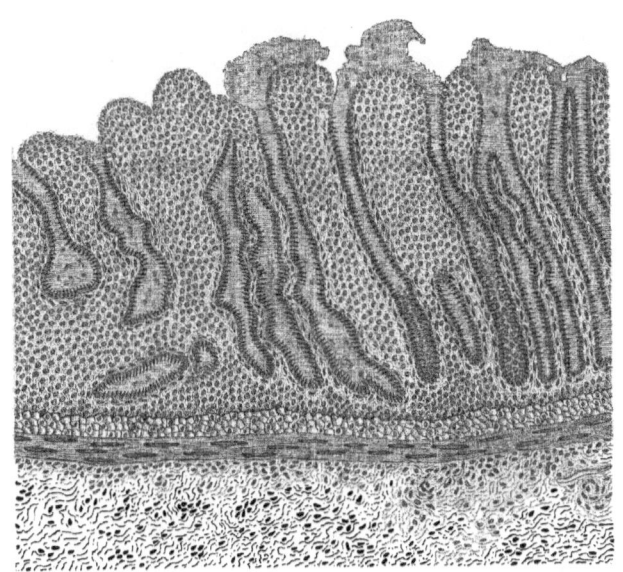

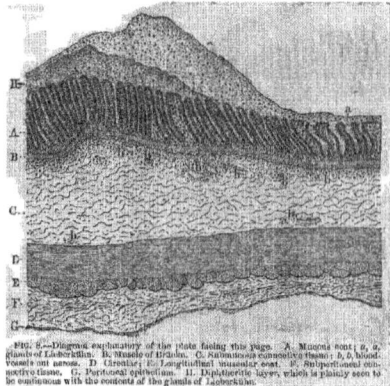

FIG. 8.—Diagram explanatory of the plate facing this page. A. Mucosa cont; a, a, glands of Lieberkühn. B. Muscle of Brücke. C. Submucous connective tissue; b, b, blood-vessels and nerves. D. Circular; E. Longitudinal muscular coat. F. Subperitoneal connective tissue. G. Peritoneal epithelium. H. Diphtheritic layer, which is plainly seen to be continuous with the contents of the glands of Lieberkühn.

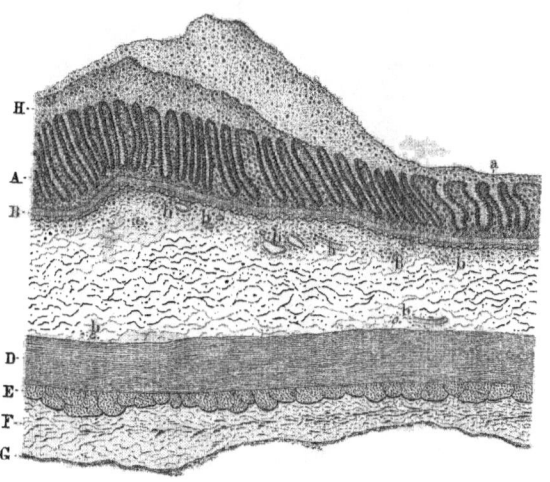

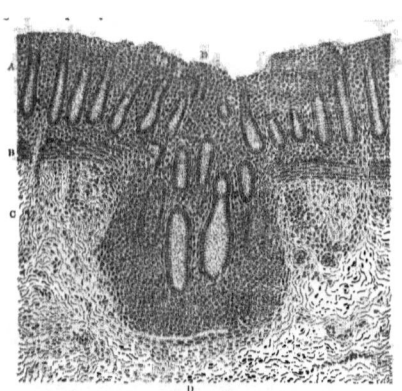

Fig. 9.—Perpendicular section of the colon of a child, cut longitudinally. Magnified 110 diameters by Powell & Lealand's ¼-inch objective. Copied from a photo-micrograph (Neg. 924, N. S.) of No. 6103. Microscopical Section. A. Mucous membrane, showing the glands of Lieberkühn pushed apart by the swarm of lymphoid elements in the adenoid tissue. B. Muscle of Brücke. C. Submucous connective tissue, with numerous lymphoid elements near the muscle of Brücke. In the centre of the piece (between D and D) is an enlarged solitary follicle in which several cystic forms, described in the text, appear. The slit-like fissure just below the enlarged gland is a lymph sinus.

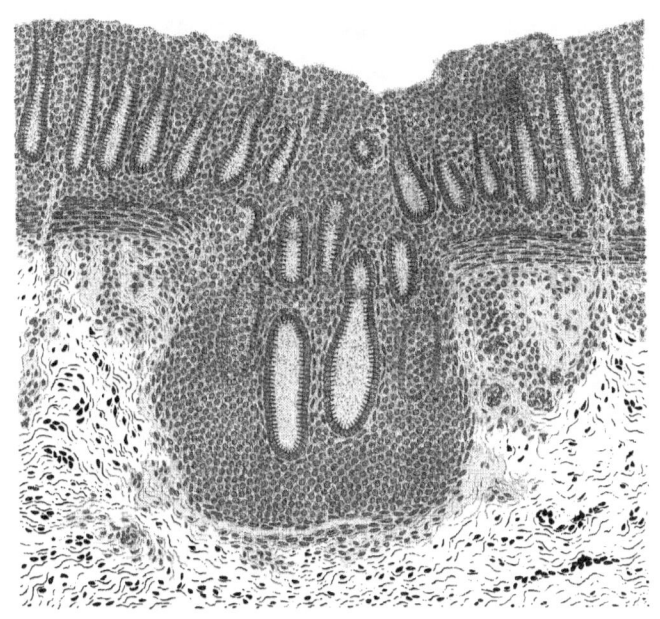

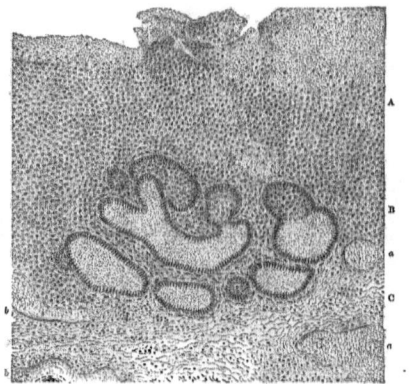

FIG. 10.—Perpendicular section of a diphtheritic colon. Magnified 110 diameters. Copied from a photo-micrograph (Neg. 998, N. S.) of No. 7260, Microscopical Section. A. Diphtheritic layer which is immediately continuous with the submucous connective tissue C. Opposite B, near the middle of the figure, are the cysts described in the text. a, a. Small veins crowded with blood corpuscles. b, b. Arteries in the submucous connective tissue.

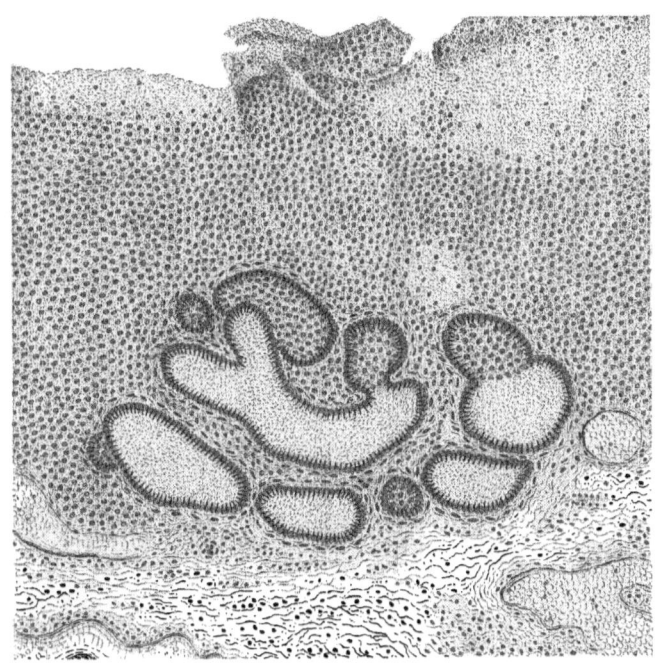

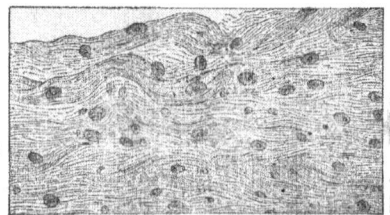

FIG. 11.—Submucous connective tissue of the colon in dysentery. Magnified 200 diameters. Copied from a photo-micrograph (Neg. 945, N. S.) of No. 7330. Microscopical Section. Lying on or between the connective-tissue bundles are two kinds of granular cells. The smaller ones without nuclei are lymphoid elements; the larger nucleated ones are the transformed parenchyma cells described in the text.

Page 468 Part II. Vol I.

FIG. 12.—Portion of the submucous connective tissue of the colon in dysentery, after teasing with needles. Magnified 200 diameters. Copied from a photomicrograph (Neg. 944, N. S.) of an extemporaneous preparation from No. 153. Medical Section. The central connective-tissue bundle shows the row of granular cells described in the text.

Page 468 Part II. Vol I.

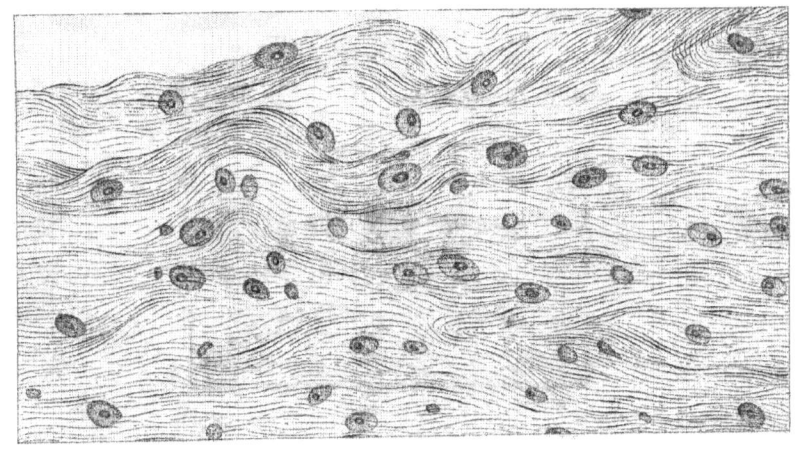

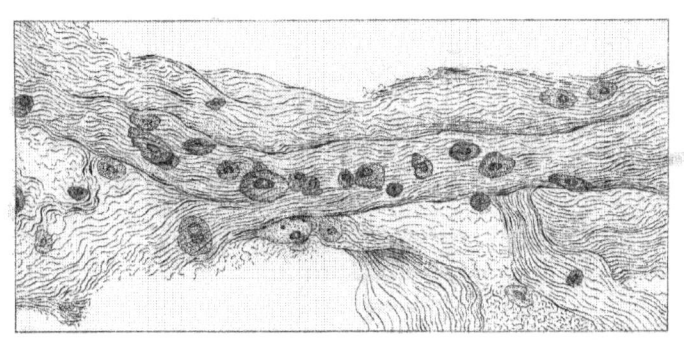

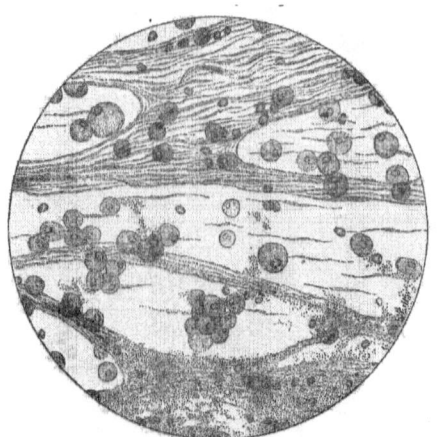

FIG. 13.—Portion of a perpendicular section through the submucous connective tissue of the ileum in a case of dysentery. Magnified 480 diameters. Copied from a photo-micrograph (Neg. 252, N. S.) of No. 7256, Microscopical Section. The lymph routes are dilated, and lying free in these and adhering to their walls are numerous rounded, granular, nucleated cells, and also a number of smaller granular bodies, (lymphoid elements.) The granules in the lower portion of the piece are micrococcus groups.

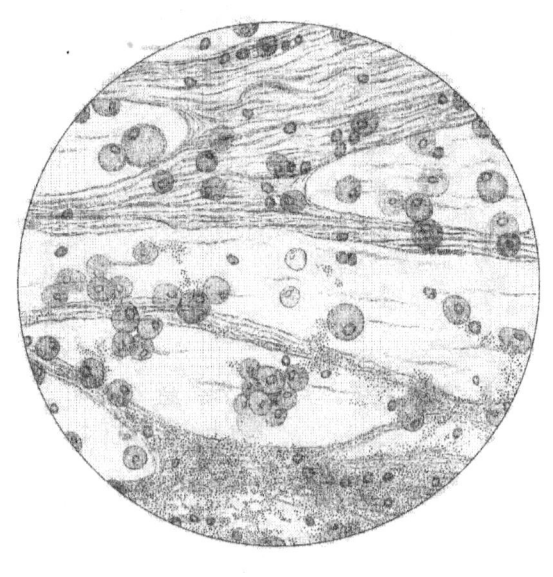

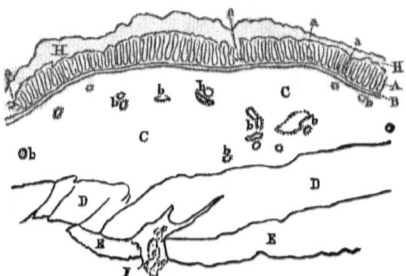

FIG. 14.—Diagram explanatory of the plate facing page 470, representing a perpendicular section of a diphtheritic colon cut transversely. A. Mucous membrane, in which *a*, *a*, *a*, *a*, are rents made by the razor. B. Muscle of Brücke. C. Thickened submucous connective tissue. *b*, *b*, *b*, *b*. Bloodvessels cut across. D. Circular. E. Longitudinal, muscular coat of the intestine. F. Point of entrance of bloodvessels. H. Diphtheritic layer.

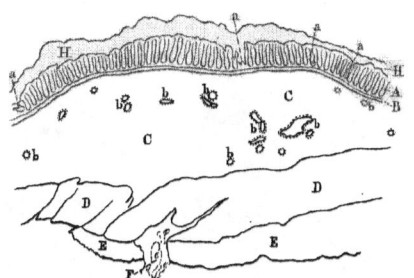

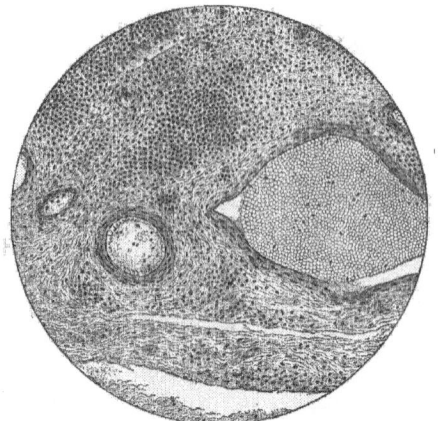

FIG. 15.—Portion of a perpendicular section through the submucous connective tissue of the colon in a case of dysentery. Magnified 175 diameters by Powell & Lealand's immersion ¼th. Copied from a photo-micrograph (Neg. 929, N. S.) of No. 7260, Microscopical Section. The nearly circular vessel to the left and below the centre of the piece is a small artery. The larger elliptical form to the right is a vein. Several smaller vessels are cut across in other parts of the piece. The connective tissue throughout is infiltrated with lymphoid elements.

Page 472 Part II. Vol. I.

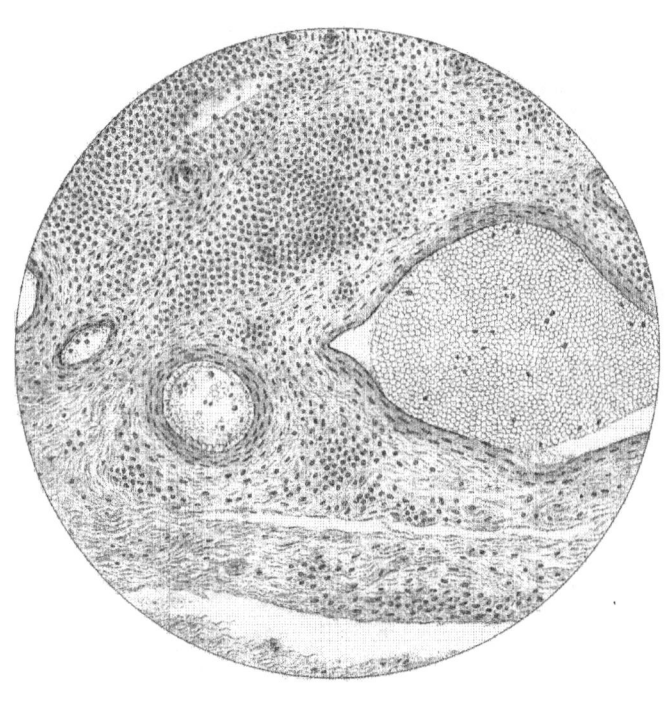

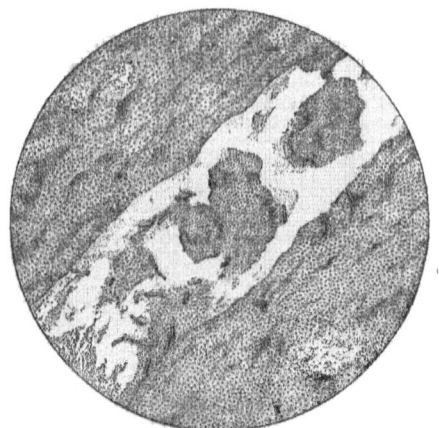

FIG. 16. Portion of a perpendicular section through the eschar in a case of diphtheritic dysentery. Magnified 550 diameters by Powell & Lealand's $\frac{1}{12}$th immersion. Copied from a photo-micrograph (Neg. 932, N. S.) of No. 7233, Microscopical Section, which is a cut of No. 72, Medical Section. The field is crossed obliquely by a cavity, (the former site of one of the glands of Lieberkühn,) in which are several micrococcus groups and a number of rod-like forms. The rest of the field is occupied with micrococcus, with a few rod-like elements near the edges of the central cavity.

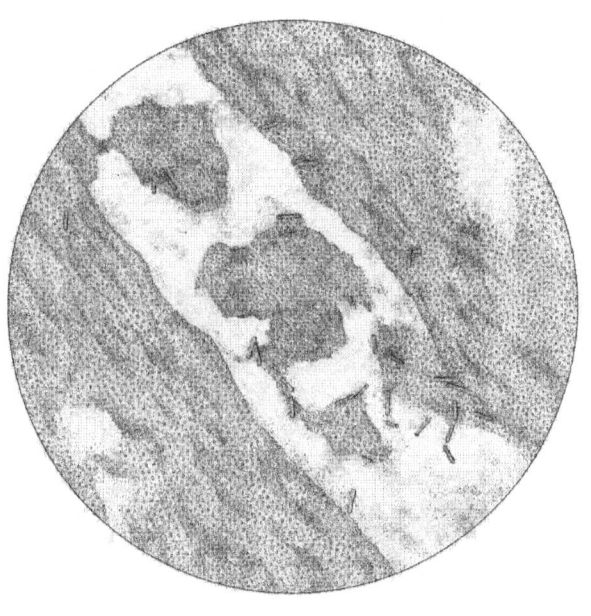

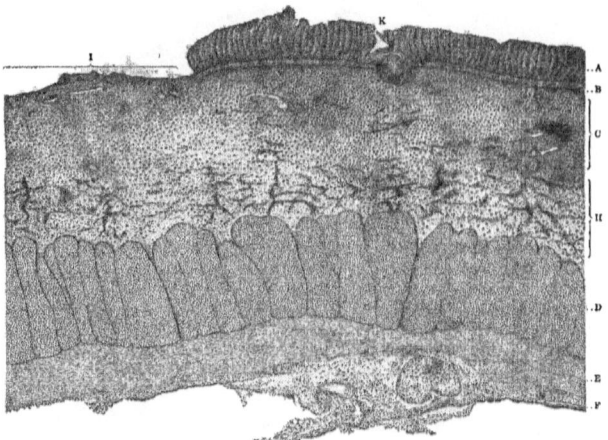

FIG. 17.—Perpendicular section of a diphtheritic colon cut longitudinally. Magnified 22 diameters. Copied from a photo-micrograph (Neg. 259, N. S.) of No. 7291, Microscopical Section, which is a cut of No. 72, Medical Section. A. Mucous membrane, a part of which, corresponding to I, has been removed by the separation of a slough. At K, an enlarged solitary follicle. The pseudomembrane layer, which coated the surface of the mucous membrane, has for the most part broken away; on the left of K a little of it still remains. B. Muscle of Brücke. C. Upper portion of the submucous connective tissue infiltrated with lymphoid elements, the size of which is considerably exaggerated in the figure. H. Lower portion of the submucous connective tissue; the dark branching figures constitute the micrococcus network. D. Circular muscular coat of the intestine. E. Longitudinal muscular coat. F. Subperitoneal connective tissue.

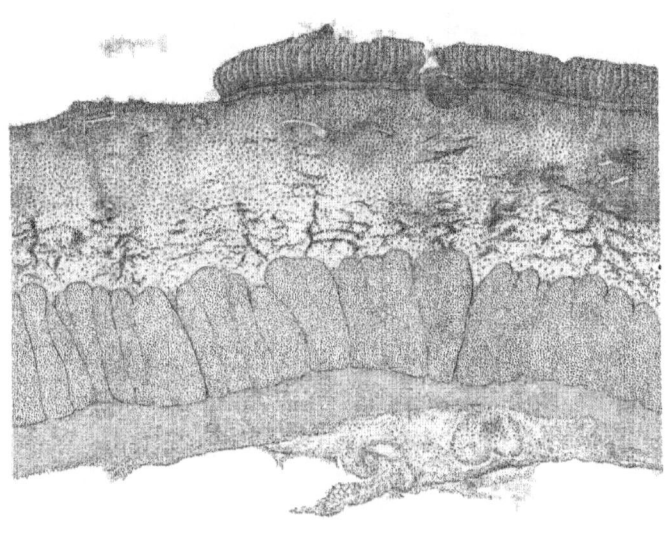

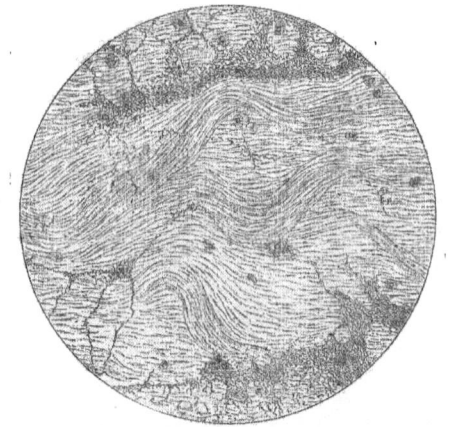

FIG. 18.—Perpendicular section of a dysenteric colon, showing the micrococcus network in the sub-mucosa. Magnified 475 diameters. Copied from a photo-micrograph (Neg. 047, N. S.) of No. 7269, Microscopical Section, which is a cut of No. 462, Medical Section. The specimen is from case 318.

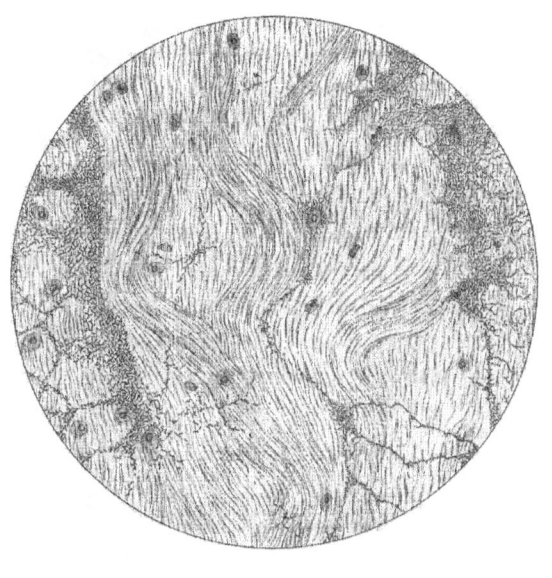

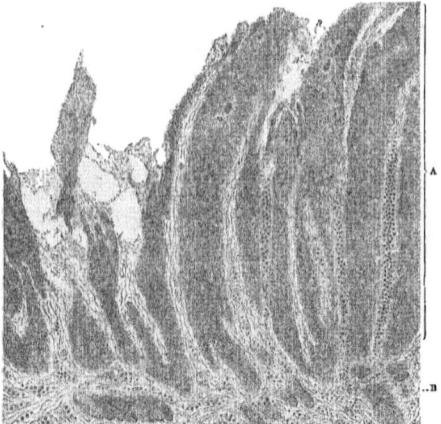

FIG. 19.—Perpendicular section of a dysenteric colon, showing sloughing of the circular muscular coat. Magnified 70 diameters. Copied from a photo-micrograph (No. 939, N. S.) of No. 7395, Microscopical Section. A. Represents the circular muscular layer which hangs in shreds into the cavity of the intestine. B. Scattered fasciuli of muscular fibre-cells belonging to the longitudinal coat, pushed apart by connective tissue infiltrated with lymphoid elements. A similar infiltrated connective tissue may be observed between the fasciculi of the circular muscular coat, especially on the right of the picture. Towards the upper part of the piece several dark oval bodies can be observed near the free extremities of the sloughs. These are the micrococcus nests described in the text; those lettered c, d, are represented as seen with a higher power in the next figure.

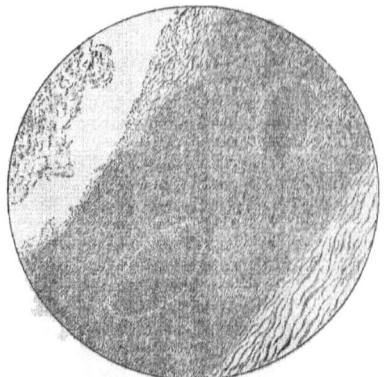

FIG. 20.—Micrococcus nests in a slough of the circular muscular coat of the intestine. Magnified 490 diameters by Powell & Lealand's ¼th immersion. Copied from a photo-micrograph. [No. 955, N. S.] The two nests represented are those marked a, d, in the last figure.

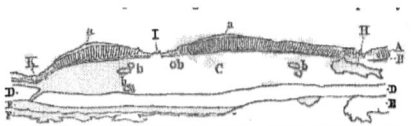

FIG. 21.—Diagram explanatory of plate facing page 480. A. Mucous membrane. a, a. Adherent pseudomembrane. B. Muscle of Brücke. C. Submucous connective tissue. b, b, b. Blood-vessels cut across. D. D. Circular. E, E. Longitudinal muscular coat. F. Subperitoneal connective tissue. H. Follicular ulcer. I. Superficial diphtheritic ulcer. K. Deep diphtheritic ulcer.

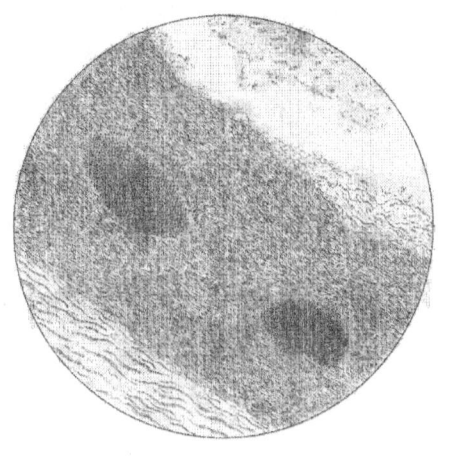

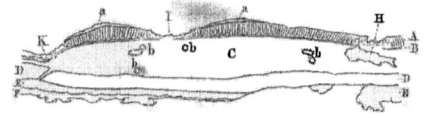

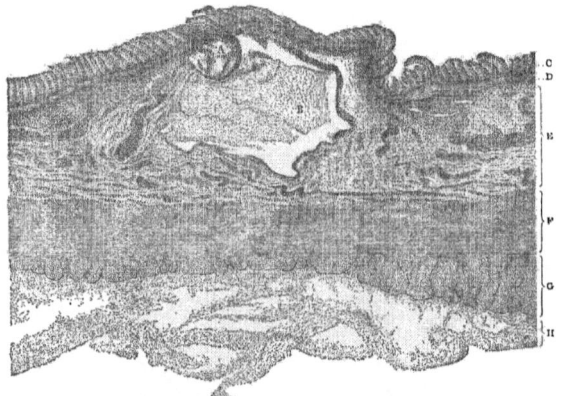

C
D

E

F

G

H

FIG. 22.—Perpendicular section through a cyst of the colon. Magnified 25 diameters by Beck's 3-inch. Copied from a photo-micrograph (Neg. 965, N. S.) of No. 7272, Microscopical Section. A, is the point at which the contents of the cyst become continuous with the lower portion of the glands of Lieberkühn. B. Glue-like mass filling the greater part of the cyst; the action of alcohol has caused it in many places to shrink away from the cyst-walls. C. Mucosa. D. Muscle of Brücke. E. Submucous connective tissue infiltrated, especially in the neighborhood of the muscle of Brücke and in the course of the venous radicles, with swarms of lymphoid cells. F. Circular muscular coat of the colon. G. Longitudinal muscular coat; on the right the edge of one of the ligamenta coli. H. Subperitoneal connective tissue.

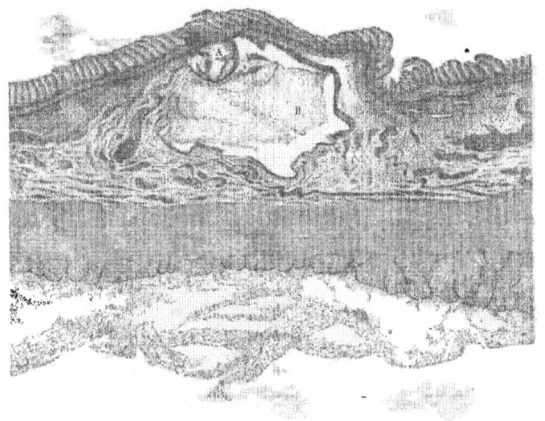

FIG. 25.—View of part of the region marked A in the section represented in the last figure, showing dilated and distorted gland tubules lined by a columnar epithelium similar to that of the glands of Lieberkühn. Magnified 200 diameters by Powell & Lealand's ⅛ immersion. Copied from a photomicrograph. (Neg. 940, N. 6.) The space between the gland tubules is filled with a granular tissue densely infiltrated with lymphoid cells. The delicate granular substance in the interior of the dilated tubules in which lymphoid elements are less numerously scattered, closely resembles the substance described in the text as filling the greater part of the eye.

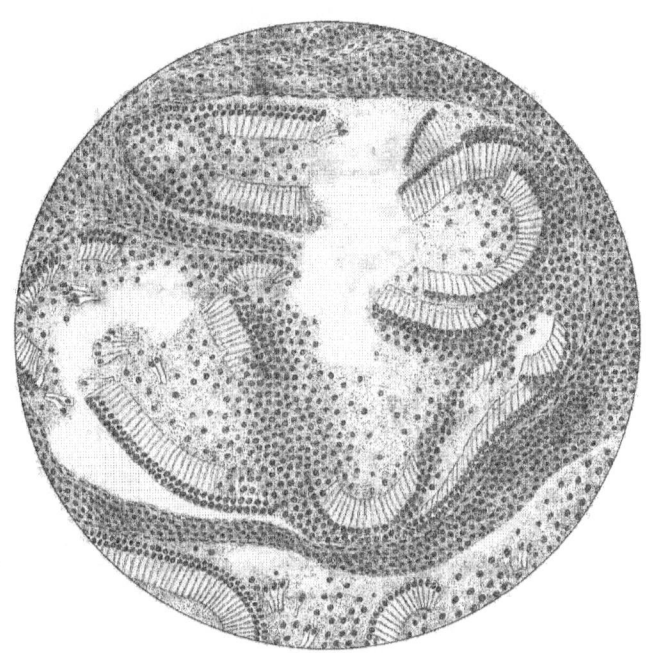

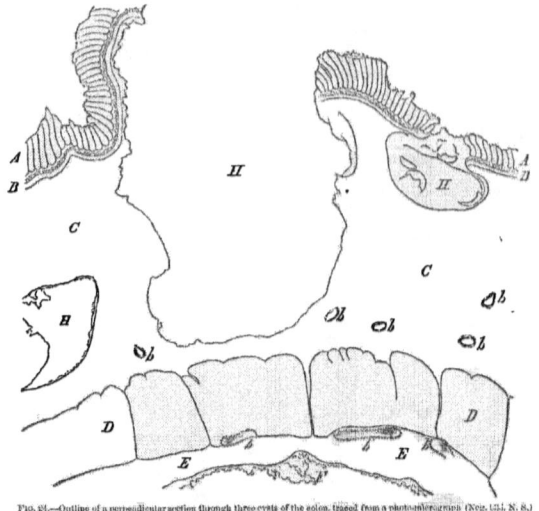

FIG. 24.—Outline of a perpendicular section through three cysts of the colon, traced from a photomicrograph (Neg. 454, N. S.) of No. 7316, Microscopical Section, (colon of case 775.) Magnified 20 diameters. A. Mucous. B. Muscle of Brücke. C. Submucous; b, b, b, b, bloodvessels cut across. D. Circular muscle of the intestine. E. Longitudinal muscle. F. Subperitoneal connective tissue. H, H, H. The three cysts described in the text.

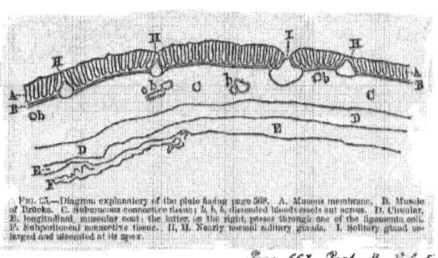

FIG. 25.—Diagram explanatory of the plate facing page 568. A. Mucous membrane. B. Muscle of Brücke. C. Submucous connective tissue; b, b, b, distended bloodvessels cut across. D. Circular, E. longitudinal, muscular coat; the latter, on the right, passes through one of the ligaments coli. F. Subperitoneal connective tissue. H, H. Nearly normal solitary glands. I. Solitary gland enlarged and ulcerated at its apex.

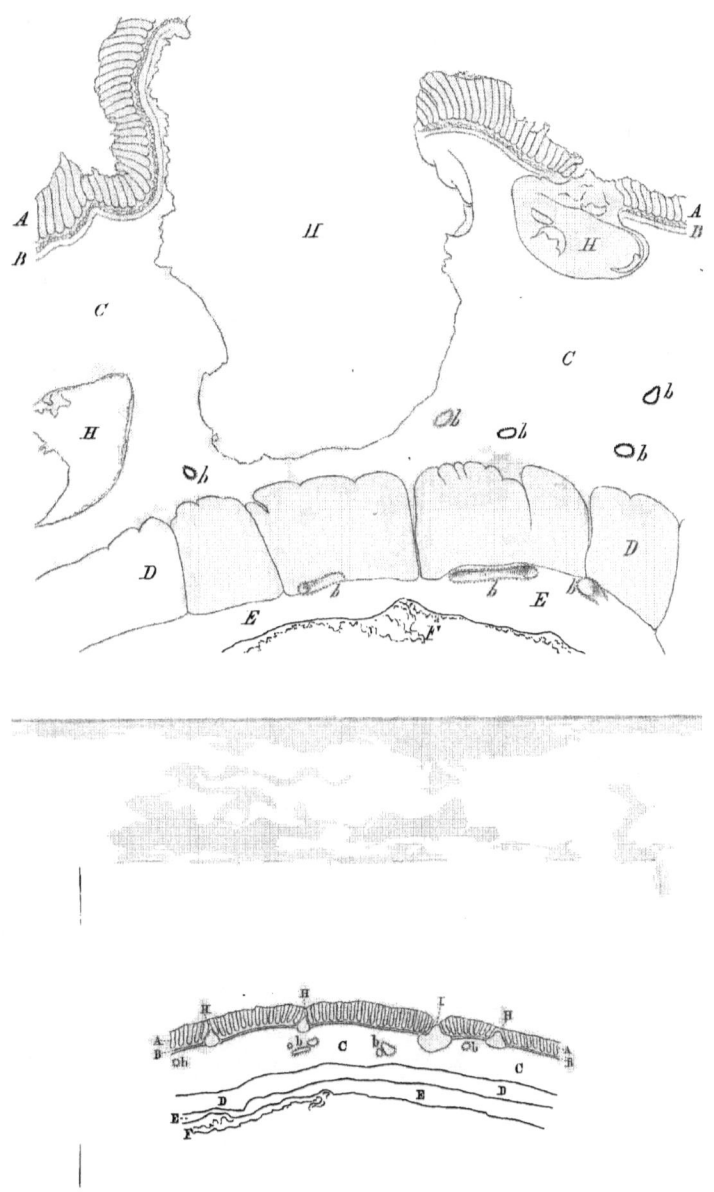

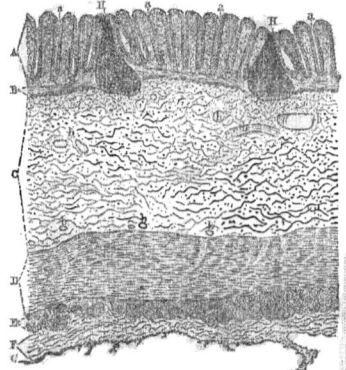

FIG. 26.—Diagram explanatory of the plate facing p. 570. A. Mucous membrane; a, a, a, a, glands of Lieberkühn. B. Muscle of Brücke. C. Submucous connective tissue infiltrated, especially near the muscle of Brücke, with lymphoid elements; b, b, b, b, bloodvessels cut across filled with coccula. D. Circular, E. longitudinal, coat of the intestine; in the latter, to the right, the cut passes through one of the ligaments cut. F. Subperitoneal connective tissue. G. Peritoneal epithelium. H. H. Two solitary follicles.

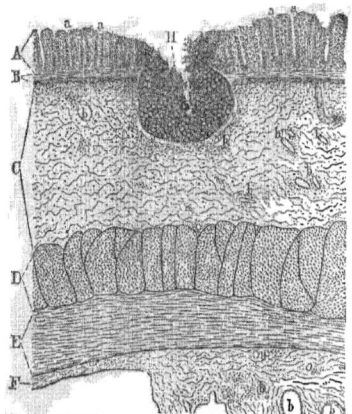

FIG. 27.—Diagram explanatory of the plate facing page 572. A. Mucous membrane; a, a, a, a, glands of Lieberkühn pushed apart by the lymphoid swarm in the normal tissue of the mucous membrane. B. Muscle of Brücke. C. Submucous connective tissue; b, b, b, b, bloodvessels cut across; c, c, lymph sinuses beneath the enlarged solitary follicle. D. Circular, E. longitudinal, muscular coat of the intestine; their arrangement shows the cut to have been a longitudinal one. F. Subperitoneal connective tissue, which, to the right of the plate, passes into the mesocolon; in the latter some bloodvessels, b, b, b, are seen cut across. H. Enlarged and ulcerated solitary gland.

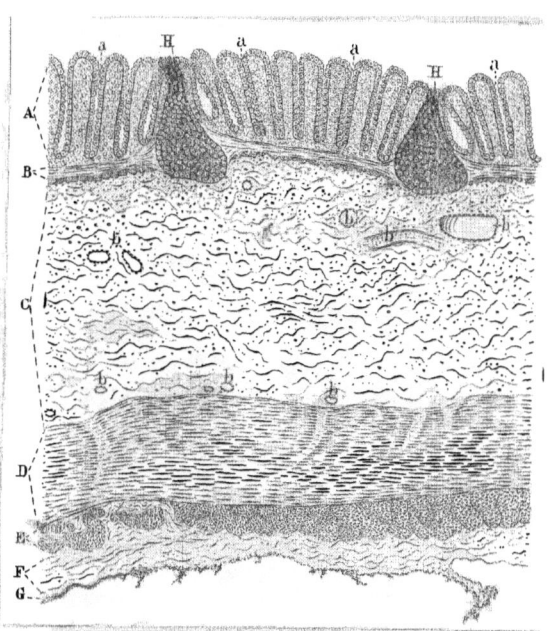

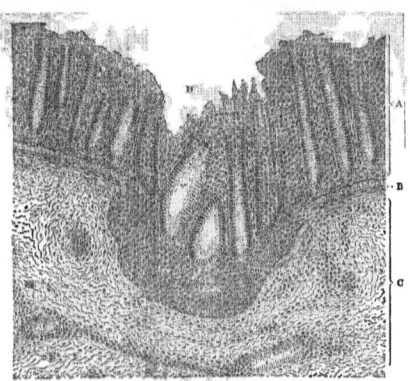

FIG. 23.—Perpendicular section of the ileum of a child, cut longitudinally. Magnified 100 diameters by Powell and Lealand's ⅕ inch objective. Copied from a photo-micrograph. (Neg. 933, N. S.) A. Mucous membrane. B. Muscle of Brücke. C. Submucous connective tissue. In the centre of the piece, below D, is an enlarged solitary gland ulcerated at its apex, and showing cystic forms in its deeper part.

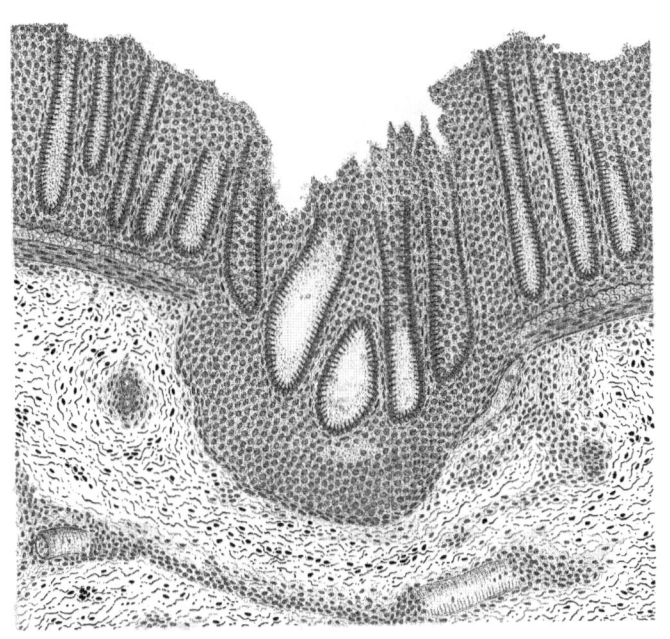

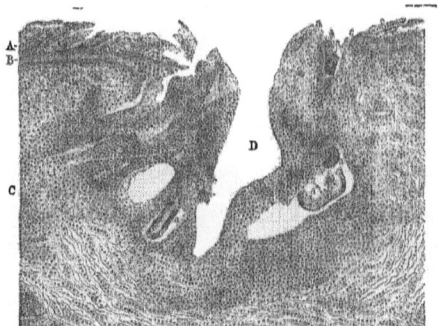

FIG. 29.—Perpendicular section through a follicular ulcer of the colon. Magnified 57 diameters. Copied from a photo-micrograph. (Neg. 354 of No. 7291), Microscopical Section, N. S.) A. Mucous membrane, its surface partly destroyed by ulceration. B. Muscle of Brucke. C. Submucous connective tissue much infiltrated with lymphoid elements. D. Cavity of follicular ulcer; a, a, a, a, gland tubules and cystic forms derived from the outgrowth of the glands of Lieberkühn. See p. 570.

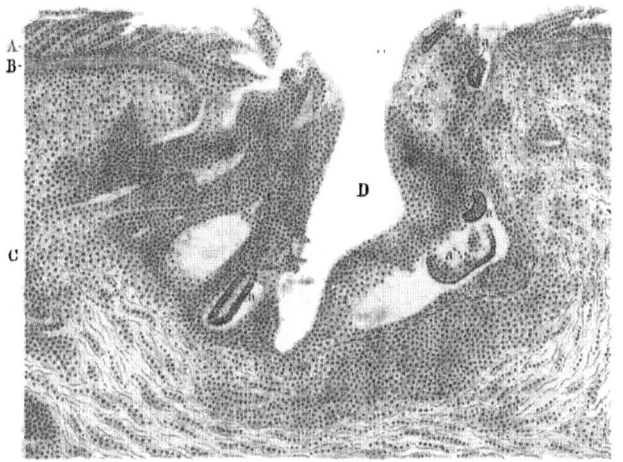

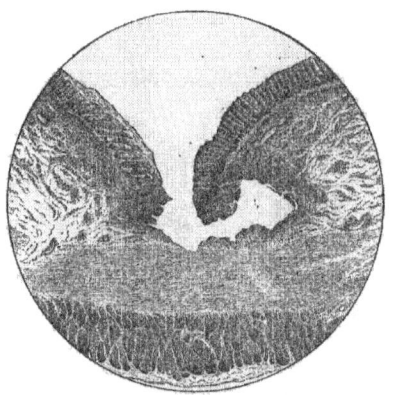

FIG. 30.—Perpendicular section through a portion of No. 6rd, Microscopical Section, showing a follicular ulcer of the colon; from a photo-micrograph, (Neg. 912, N. S.) The scale is in 1/10 and 1/100 of an inch. See p. 571.

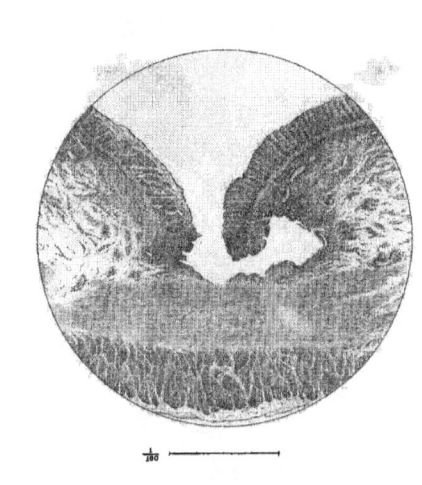

$\frac{1}{100}$ |————————|

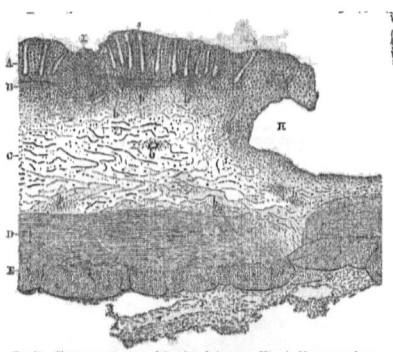

FIG. 31.—Diagram explanatory of the plate facing page 574. A. Mucous membrane; a, a, glands of Lieberkühn pushed apart by the infiltration of the adenoid tissue with lymphoid elements. B. Muscle of Brücke. C. Submucous connective tissue; b, b, b, distended bloodvessels cut across; c, lymph sinus. D. Circular, E. longitudinal, layers of the muscular coat of the intestine. F. Subperitoneal connective tissue. H. Cavity of a follicular ulcer. I. Solitary follicle at the apex of which ulceration has just commenced. See p. 572.

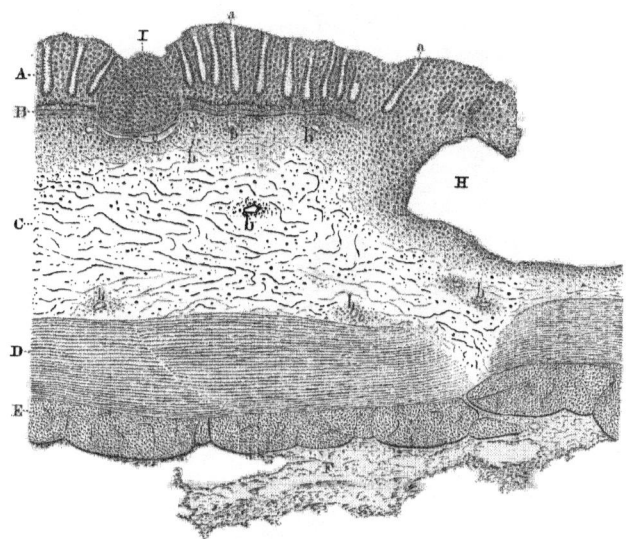

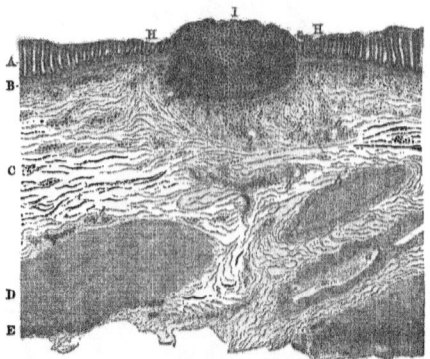

FIG. 32.—Perpendicular section of the colon from case 310, showing a small superficial ulcer H, H, in the centre of which an intact solitary follicle, I, protrudes as a minute nipple-like elevation. Half-diagrammatic drawing from a photograph (Neg. 363, N. 8.) of No. 933. Microscopical Section. Magnified 66 diameters. A. Mucous membrane. H. Muscle of Brücke. C. Submucous connective tissue; b, b, b, small veins cut across. D. Circular, E. Longitudinal, muscular coats of the intestine; these are divided by the entrance of an artery, a, from the mesocolon, which is accompanied by a vein of considerable size and surrounded with connective tissue.

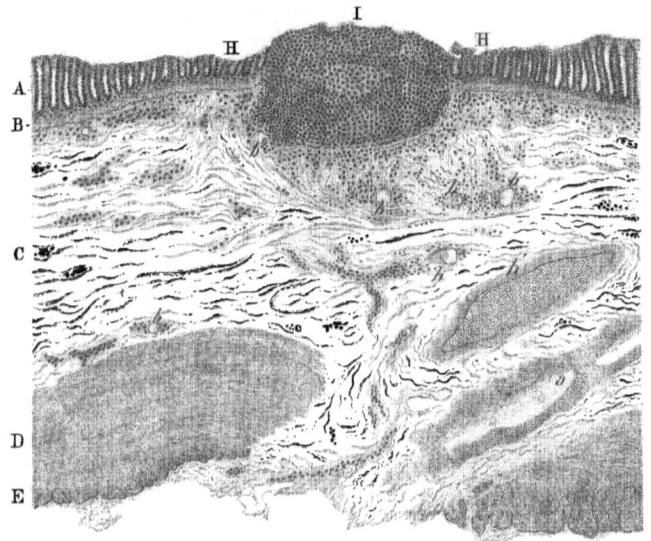

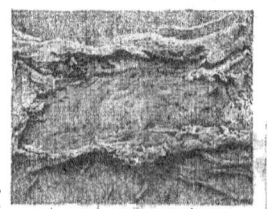

FIG. 33.—Tubercular girdle-sore, natural size. From a photograph of No. 429, Medical Section, Army Medical Museum. (Case 413.) See p. 584.

Page 583, Part II. Vol I.

FIG. 34.—A number of small tubercular ulcers in a very slightly thickened Peyer's patch, natural size. From a photograph of No. 430, Medical Section, Army Med. Museum.

Page 584, Part II. Vol. I.

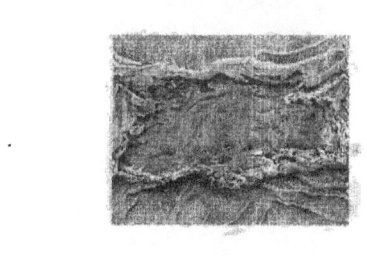

FIG. 35.—Tubercular ulcer of the cæcum, natural size. From a photograph of No. 431, Medical Section, Army Medical Museum.

Page 584. Part II. Vol. I.

FIG. 36.—Tubercular ulcers of the ileum, natural size. From a photograph of No. 770, Medical Section, Army Medical Museum.

Page 585. Part II. Vol. I.

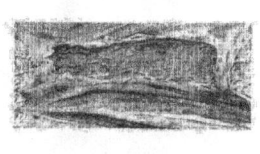

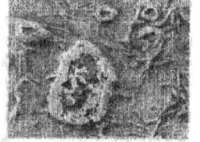

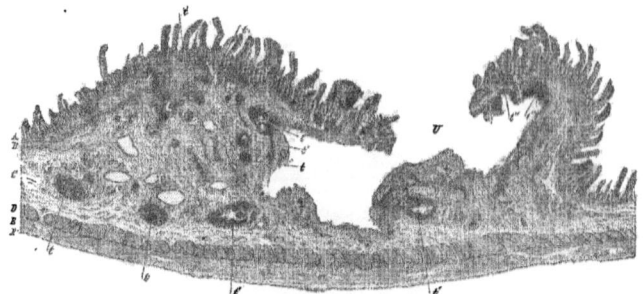

FIG. 57.—Perpendicular section through a small tubercular ulcer of the ileum. Magnified 15 diameters. From a photo-micrograph [Neg. 978, N. S.] of No. 7340. Microscopical Section, from case 413. A. The mucous membrane, with its tubular glands pushed apart by the accumulation of lymphoid elements; its villi greatly hypertrophied. B. The muscle of Brücke. C. Submucous connective tissue infiltrated with lymphoid elements, containing a number of tubercles in various stages; its bloodvessels dilated. D. Circular muscular coat of the intestine. E. Longitudinal muscular coat. F. Peritoneum. U. Cavity of the ulcer. *t, t, t, t, t.* Unsoftened tubercles. The two letters below the lower edge point to tubercles, in the centres of which growing axial forms are seen, (lymphatic vessels cut across? gland cells?) the nature of which will be discussed further on. There are besides several unsoftened tubercles which are not lettered. *t', t', t', t'.* Tubercles with central softening in which part of the cheesy mass has fallen out. *t'', t''.* Softened tubercles whose cavities form part of the ulcer.

Page 567. Part II. Vol 1.

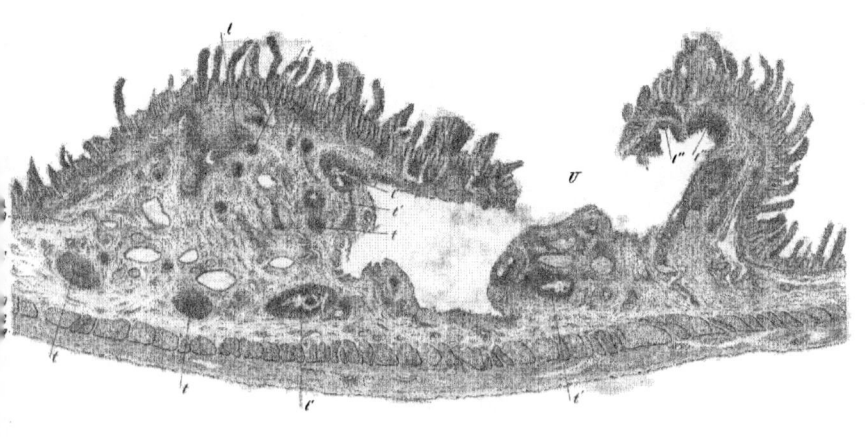

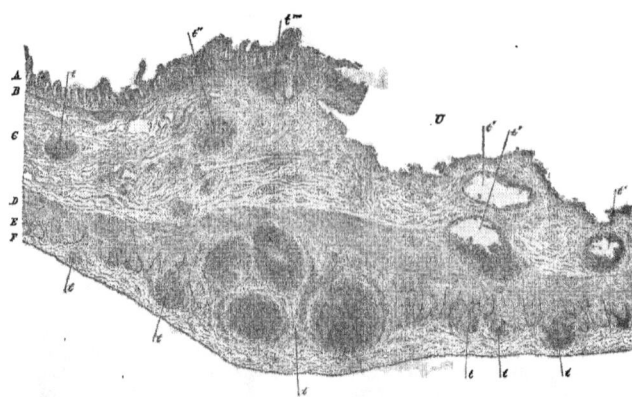

FIG. 38.—Perpendicular section cut transversely through the edge of a tubercular girdle-sore of the ileum. From a photo-micrograph [Neg. 978, N. S.] of No. 7519, Microscopical Section. A. Mucous membrane; its tubular glands pushed apart by an accumulation of lymphoid elements in the adenoid tissue; its villi hypertrophied, but most of them accidentally broken off in making the section. B. The muscle of Brücke. C. Submucous connective tissue, infiltrated with lymphoid elements, especially in the vicinity of the muscle of Brücke and near the edges of the ulcer; its bloodvessels dilated; it contains also a number of tubercles. D. Circular muscular coat of the intestine. E. Longitudinal muscular coat. F. Subperitoneal connective tissue, much thickened, and containing tubercles. t, t, t, t, t, t. Tubercles; there are also several not lettered; near the centre of the lower edge of the section five tubercles grouped together form a compound one. t′, t′, t′. Softened tubercles from whose interior the cheesy mass has dropped out in making the section. t″. A tubercle containing one of the peculiar bodies alluded to in the description of Fig. 37. t′″. A tubercle in the substance of which a vascular loop (arteriole?) can be clearly seen. Such vessels ultimately cease to be permeable. Magnified 20 diameters.

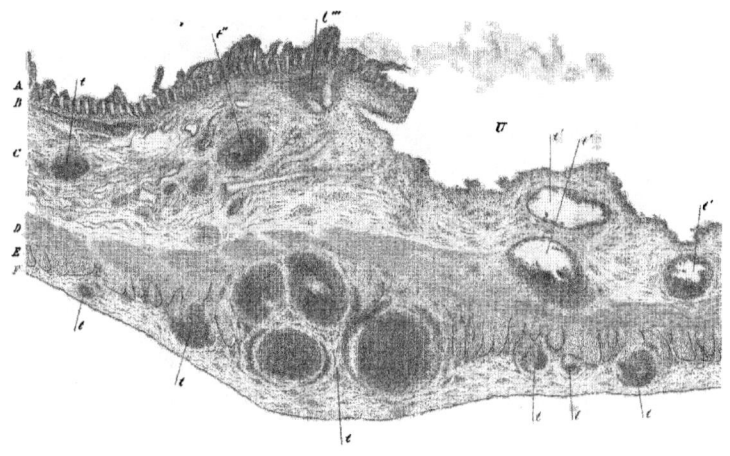

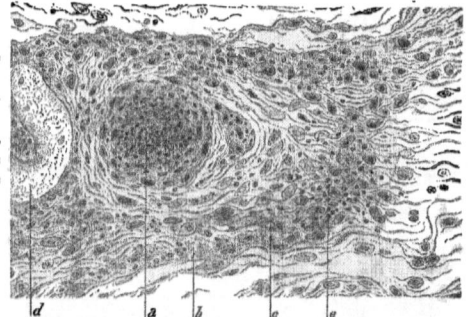

FIG. 39.—Small tubercle in the submucosa of the ileum. From the same case as Fig. 37. Magnified 370 diameters by Powell & Lealand's immersion 1/15. Copied from a photo-micrograph (Neg. 366, N. S.) of a part of No. 7341, Microscopical Section. a, Central figure (lymphatic) cut across; it is stuffed with granular fibrin, in which lymphoid elements, and on the periphery endothelial cells, are imbedded; indications of the limiting wall and of a small branch are also seen. In the space around the central figure are numerous granular nucleated endothelial cells like that indicated at b. In one of these cells, c, a vacuole has formed. There are also numerous lymphoid elements; a group of four is indicated at c. A small vein, d, passes through the margin of the tubercle. Traces of a fibrillated connective-tissue matrix are seen everywhere, outside of the central figure, between the elements.

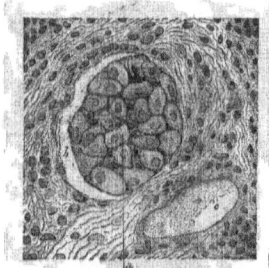

FIG. 40.—Transverse section through the lumen of a diseased lymphatic vessel in the submucosa of the ileum. Same case as Fig. 37. Magnified 620 diameters by Powell & Lealand's immersion 1/15th. Copied from a photo-micrograph (Neg. 369, N. S.) of a part of No. 7341, Microscopical Section. The lumen of the vessel was filled with a mass of large endothelial cells, (a,) between which a few lymphoid elements have crept. In preparing the specimen this mass has shrunk away from the wall of the vessel, leaving a space, b. In the neighborhood of this stuffed lymphatic the section passes through a venous radicle, c. The surrounding connective tissue is infiltrated with lymphoid elements and presents also a few large endothelial cells.

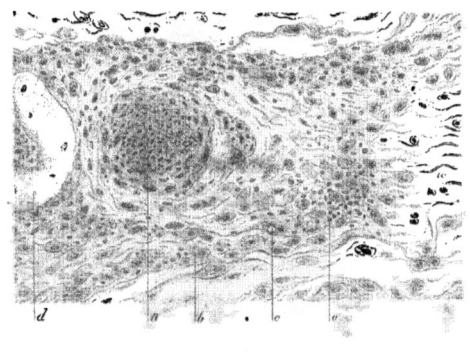

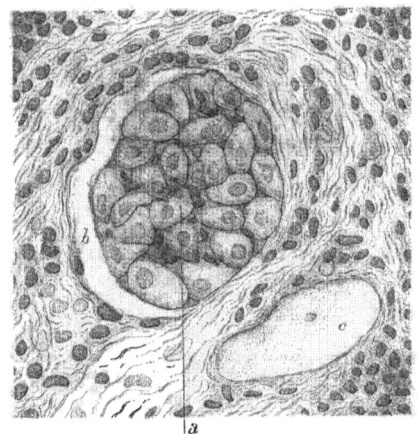

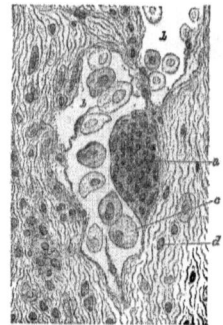

FIG. 41.—Section through the lumen of a lymphatic in the submucosa of the ileum. Same case as Fig. 37. Magnified 480 diameters by Powell & Lealand's immersion 1/8th. Copied from a photomicrograph (Neg. 165, N. S.) of a part of No. 7541, Microscopical Section. A granular fibrin-clot, a, in which both lymphoid and endothelial elements are imbedded, adheres on one side to the walls of a lymphatic vessel, in whose lumen, b, b, basemed endothelial elements lie free. Similar elements appear in the connective tissue surrounding the vessel, with a number of lymphoid elements, one of which is indicated at d. See p. 594.

Page 595. Path M⁻ Vol. I.

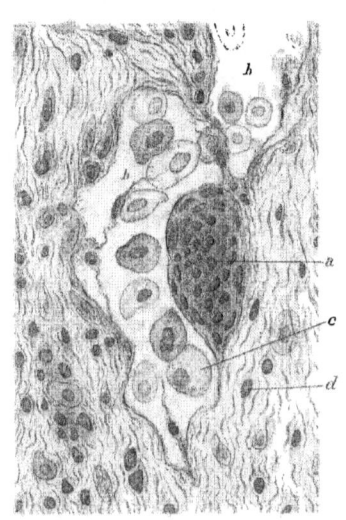

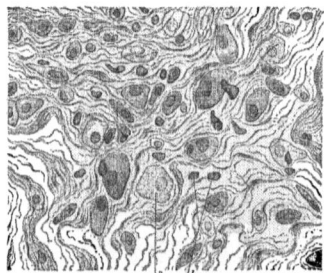

FIG. 43.—Portion of the submucosa of the ileum from the same case as Fig. 37. Magnified 480 diameters by Powell & Lealand's immersion ¼ in. Copied from a photo-micrograph (Neg. 267, N. S.) of a part of No. 7591, Microscopical Section. In the meshes of the fibrillated matrix there are a number of large granular nucleated cells (transformed connective-tissue corpuscles, endothelial cells,) one of which is indicated by *a*, and numerous smaller lymphoid elements, two of which are indicated by *b*. See p. 595.

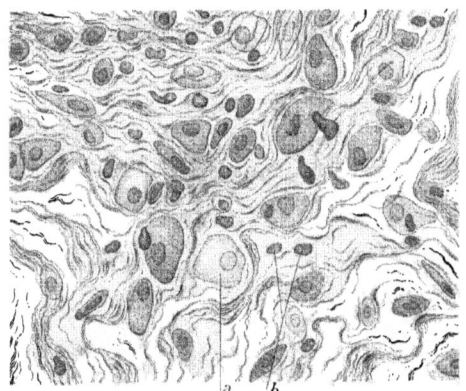